ALLEY CATS

A collection of kitty tales

Written by Lesley Rees

Illustrated by Terry Burton

This is a Parragon Book
This edition published in 2001
PARRAGON, Queen Street House, 4 Queen Street, Bath
BA1 1HE, UK

Copyright © PARRAGON 2000

Created and produced by THE COMPLETE WORKS

Printed in China

ISBN 0-75256-636-9

Contents

Sports Day

The sun peeped over the higgledy-piggledy, messy alley. It was much too early to be awake—or was it?

Lenny the kitten slowly opened his eyes and grinned—it was 'time-to-get-up' time.

"Get up, Sleepyhead!" he yelled to his twin sister, Lulu. "It's a great day for running and jumping." And he started to run round and round the trash cans.

"Okay, Lenny," yawned Lulu, still half asleep, "I'm coming."

"I'll race you to the end of the alley," cried Lenny.

"But you always win," moaned Lulu.

"That's because you're a big, plump kitty," laughed Lenny.

Lulu giggled. "Naughty kitty!" she cried. "Bet you can't catch me!" And she ran down the alley as fast as she could.

"That was fun!" cried Lenny, as he finally caught up with his sister. "What about some jumping now?"

"Great idea," purred Lulu.

So, huffing and puffing, the little kittens piled up some boxes and put a pole across the gap.

Lenny leapt over it first. "Whee!" he cried. "I bet I can jump higher than you!"

Suddenly, Lulu spotted a raggedy old ball.

"I bet I can throw it further than you!" she cried.

"No, you can't," cried Lenny. He picked up the ball and threw his best throw ever—but it hit Uncle Bertie right on the head!

Scampering down the alley as fast as they could go, the two kittens quickly hid behind a heap of old potato sacks before Uncle Bertie could spot them!

"Pooh!" said Lulu. "These sacks are really smelly!"

Suddenly, Lenny had an idea...

Pulling one of the old potato sacks up to his tummy, he began hopping and jumping around!

"Hey, what about a sack race?" he giggled.

Lenny hopped and skipped. Lulu wiggled and giggled.

"I'm winning!" squealed Lulu. "I'm winning!"

"No, you're not!" cried Lenny. He jumped his best jump ever — and knocked a huge pile of boxes over Cousin Archie!

"Uh-oh!" groaned Lenny. "Trouble time!"

Uncle Bertie and Cousin Archie were not happy. They stomped off to find Hattie, the kitten's mother.

"Those kittens of yours are *so* naughty," they complained. "You've got to do something about them!"

Hattie sighed. Then, spying two pairs of tiny ears peeping out from behind a watering can, she tip-toed over. "Time-to-come-out-time!" she boomed.

23

"What have you two been up to?" Hattie asked Lenny and Lulu.

"Running and jumping, Mommy," whined Lenny.

"We didn't mean to hurt anyone," whispered Lulu.

But Hattie wasn't cross. She knew her kittens were only playing. "I've got an idea," she said. "Why don't we have a sports day? We can all join in—there'll be plenty of running and jumping for everyone!"

Archie and Bertie didn't want to play—they wanted a cat nap!

"Okay," said Hattie. "We'll simply ask the dogs to join us instead."

So, later that day, Hattie explained her idea to the Alley Dogs, who all thought it sounded like great fun. And it wasn't long before Hattie had organised everyone and everything!

"We'll have lots of races," cried Lenny, excitedly, "running, skipping, leaping and jumping ones— maybe even a sack race!"

Suddenly, six kitty eyes peeped over the fence.

"Okay, everyone," cried Hattie. "Let's begin.

Ready... steady... "

"Er, Hattie," asked Cousin Archie, popping out from behind the fence, "can I join in?"

"Us too?" cried Uncle Bertie and Auntie Lucy.

"Of course you can," laughed Hattie.

"Ready... steady... GO!"

Cousin Archie and Harvey raced up the alley and passed the winning line together. "Archie and Harvey are the winners!" cried Hattie. "Time for the sack race now!"

The dogs and cats all clambered into their sacks. But Lenny and Lulu began before Hattie could say "Go!"

"Hey!" cried Hattie, "come back you two, that's cheating!" But it was too late. Everyone began leaping and jumping after the kittens.

"STOP!" shouted Hattie.

Lenny and Lulu stopped – but no one else did! They crashed into each other and fell in a big Alley Dog and Cat pickle!

Luckily, no-one was hurt, but now they were all tired.

"Well, that was the best sports day ever!" said Harvey.

Hattie looked at the higgledy-piggledy mess.

34

"You're right," she laughed. "But tomorrow we're going to play another game. It's called tidy-up the alley!"

Suddenly, lots of barking and meowing filled the air. "Oh, no!" they groaned, and then they all laughed.

Birthday Surprise

In the higgledy-piggledy, messy alley, the sun
was just beginning to shine. It was very early.
Even the birds hadn't begun to chirp and cheep
yet. Everyone and everything was fast asleep.
Or were they?

41

Slowly, a sleepy head peeped out of a trash can. It was Uncle Bertie.

First he opened one eye… then the other…
and gave a great big grin!

"It's here, at last!" he chuckled to himself.

"Happy Birthday to me! Happy Birthday to me!" he sang, at the top of his voice. He looked around, but no one had heard. Everyone was still snoozing and snoring! Didn't they know it was his birthday?

"Time-to-get-up-time!" he shouted, as he banged on a trash can lid — **CLANG! CLANG! CLANG!**

Lenny and Lulu, the two kittens, fell out of their basket in fright. Cousin Archie tumbled off his branch, right on top of poor Hattie!

46

"Uncle Bertie!" snapped Hattie, the kitten's mother, "why are you bashing that trash can lid?"

"Sorry!" said Uncle Bertie. "Er… it's just that it's my… er… well, it's time-to-get-up-time!"

"Oh, Bertie!" sighed Hattie. Now she was awake, she decided to get up and get her kittens ready. How they wriggled and wiggled—they hated wash time!

Cousin Archie scritched and scratched his claws on an old mat. Auntie Lucy just rolled over and went back to sleep! Poor Uncle Bertie! How sad he looked. Wasn't anyone going to wish him a happy birthday?

"Do you know what day it is today, Hattie?" he asked.

"Yes, Bertie," she replied.

"Is it a special day?" Bertie asked, hopefully.

"No, it's just a normal Tuesday," replied Hattie. "Now run along, I've got breakfast to make."

Then Bertie spotted the twins chasing a butterfly.

"Hey, you two!" he called. "Bet you don't know what day it is today."

"Of course we do," said Lulu. "It's Saturday!"

"It's not, Loony Lulu!" said Lenny and pushed his sister into a puddle!

"Oh, Lenny!" cried Lulu. "I'm telling Mommy!"

"No, twins," said Uncle Bertie, "it's my... "

But the naughty kittens were already halfway down the alley.

Suddenly, Archie jumped out from behind a box.

"Hello, Cousin Archie," said Bertie. "Bet you don't know what today is!"

"Bet I do," said Archie, with a grin.

"What is it then?" asked Bertie.

"I'm not telling!" giggled Archie and scampered off down the alley. "It's for me to know and you to find out!"

"But I do know!" cried Bertie. "It's my *birthday*!"

But Archie was already gone.

"I know who will remember!" said Bertie.
"Harvey, the Alley Dog will—he knows
everything!" And he rushed up the alley
to find him.

"Hello, guys," called Bertie to the dogs. "Guess what
today is?"

"Snack day?" rumbled Ruffles, the Old English Sheepdog.

"Christmas day?" woofed Puddles, the puppy.

"No!" meowed Bertie, crossly. "Doesn't anyone know? It's…"

"Chasing Bertie day!" barked Harvey and started to run after him.

Bertie ran down the alley and jumped over the fence into the orchard.

"I don't care anyway!" he sulked. "Who wants a rotten old birthday?"

Poor Bertie didn't see the five pairs of cats' eyes peeping over the fence. And he didn't hear five kitties, planning and giggling!

"This is the worst birthday ever!" wailed Bertie.

"Tee-hee," whispered Cousin Archie. "Looks as though our plan is working!"

"I need to find the Alley Dogs," purred Hattie and clambered down from the fence.

Luckily, Harvey was already there!

"Is everything ready?" she asked. Harvey smiled and nodded his head.

Back in the orchard, Uncle Bertie was fed up.
He decided to go home and have a sleep.
He squeezed through the tiny gap in the fence.

"SURPRISE!" yelled the Alley Cats and Dogs. The alley was decorated with bright, colorful streamers. There was even a cake in the shape of a fish! Bertie was so happy!

"You remembered!" said Bertie.

"Oh, Bertie," said Hattie, "how could we forget!" She gave him a big hug.

"Thanks, gang!" grinned Bertie. "This is the best birthday ever!"

The End

Little Lost Lenny

One gray day, Lenny, the kitten, was happily chasing his twin sister, Lulu, around the higgledy-piggledy, messy alley. They were having great fun, leaping over boxes and jumping through tires.

Hattie, their mommy, looked up at the big, dark clouds.
"I think we had better tidy up before it rains," she said.
"Come on, everyone, let's put everything away."

So Uncle Bertie and Cousin Archie
moved the boxes.

Auntie Lucy helped Hattie tidy away the blankets. Even little Lulu helped by clearing away her toys – she didn't want the rain to make them squelchy and soggy!

Everyone was busy helping... or were they?

73

That little mischief-maker, Lenny, was planning something naughty! He hid behind Lulu's trash can, then leapt out and snatched her teddy.

With a giggle, he ran off down the alley. Lulu gave a long wail. Teddy was her favorite toy.

"Mommy!" she yelled. "Lenny's got my teddy!"

Lenny stopped at the bottom of the alley and called to his sister.

"If you want Teddy," he said, "come and get him."

Lulu raced down the alley.

Lenny giggled and tossed the teddy
high into the sky.

He went straight over his sister's head
and disappeared behind a large fence!

Lulu stood and wailed until all the other cats came charging down the alley.

Lenny knew he was going to be in *big* trouble.

"Whatever's the matter?" cried Hattie.
The little kitten sobbed and told her
mommy what her naughty brother had done.

Everyone looked at Lenny.

"Lenny, you really are a naughty kitty!" said his mother, crossly. "You know you're not supposed to come down to this part of the alley."

Bertie scooped up Lulu. "Don't worry," he said, kindly.
"Archie and I will find Teddy for you later."

Lenny stood still, bit his lip and trembled.

"Why do you have to get into so much trouble?" asked Hattie. "And why can't you be more helpful like your sister?" And off she stomped, back towards her trash can.

"Sorry, Mommy," whispered Lenny.

A big, fat tear trickled down his cheek.

"It's not fair," he thought. "I didn't mean to lose silly old Teddy!"

Lenny gave a sniff and wandered over to the gate. He peeped through the bars. Mommy had said that they must never, *ever* go through this gate.

"But I don't know why," thought Lenny.

"I do know that Teddy's in there, though,"
he said, "and I must try and get him back."

So he squeezed himself through the bars…

Lenny found himself standing at the edge of a big building site. There were wooden planks and piles of bricks everywhere— Lenny thought it looked great fun.

"I don't know why Mommy told me to keep away from here," he laughed. "It's like having my very own adventure playground."

The naughty kitty soon
forgot about feeling sad as he
climbed ladders and walked
across gangplanks, high above
the ground.

"I'm Lucky Lenny the Pirate!"
he laughed. Then he stopped
and peered through the rain.

"And there's Teddy!" he cried.

87

As Lenny grabbed the bear, the plank tipped up.

The rain had made it very slippery and…

down,

down,

down

he fell —
all the way
to the bottom
of a mucky,
muddy hole.

Luckily, cats always
land on their feet,
so he wasn't hurt,
but he'd had
a real fright!

Lenny's little claws tried to grip the sides of the hole, but the rain had loosened the soil. It sprinkled down all over his head!

Oh dear, now he really *was* stuck!

"Mommy! Mommy!" he meowed. "**Help!**"

Meanwhile, back in the alley, the cats were sheltering from the rain. Suddenly, Hattie looked round.

"Where's Lenny?" she asked the others. But no-one had seen him for ages.

Hattie ran out into the alley. "Lenny!" she cried through the pouring rain. "Lenny, where are you?"

She knew something was wrong.

"Go and get the dogs," she said to Archie. "Ask them to help us find my poor, little Lenny."

Archie quickly returned with Harvey and the gang.

"Don't worry, Hattie," said Harvey. "We'll soon find him for you."

All the dogs and cats ran out into the pouring rain, meowing and barking Lenny's name.

At the bottom of the alley, the Old English Sheepdog, Ruffles, sniffed.

"I can smell him!" he yelped. "He's very near!"

He snuffled to the gate. "Yes, he's in there!" cried Patchy, the dog with a patch over one eye, "I can hear him crying!"

The animals rushed through the gate and quickly found the muddy hole where Lenny was stuck.

"Don't worry!" called Harvey. "We'll soon get you out."

Uncle Bertie found a thick rope. "We can use this," he called.

Ruffles, Harvey and Bertie lowered the rope to Lenny. The tiny kitten clung on tight and was pulled to safety.

Lenny gave Teddy back to Lulu. "I didn't mean to make you sad," he said.

"We were *so* worried!" said Hattie. "No special kitty treats for you tonight.

"I'm really sorry, Mommy," sniffed Lenny.

Hattie smiled and gave her naughty, little kitten a big hug. "That's okay," she smiled. "At least you're safe now." Then, all the Alley Cats went back to the alley for lots of cat-napping!

The sun was shining in the higgledy-piggledy, messy alley.

"It's much too hot!" Hattie thought to herself, as she tried to find a nice shady spot for a snooze. Her kittens, Lenny and Lulu, were cat-napping under the apple tree and she knew from the loud snoring that Uncle Bertie and Auntie Lucy were fast asleep in their trash cans. Everyone was hiding from the sun — everyone except Cousin Archie!

Archie was lying on top of the fence,
slurping his third bottle of milk!

He didn't notice the sun's rays shining through the glass of those empty milk bottles. It was focused right onto Hattie's trash can full of old newspapers—the perfect place for a fire to start!

Suddenly, Hattie's nose twitched.

"What's that?" she wondered. "It smells like smoke."

"It is smoke!" she gasped, as she saw bright red and yellow flames leaping out of her trash can.

"F-Fire!" she cried. "Help!"

"Wake up, Bertie!" cried Hattie. "My trash can's on fire!"

Uncle Bertie's sleepy head popped up from his dustbin.

"I must have been dreaming, Hattie!" he yawned.
"I dreamt that your trash was on fire."

"It wasn't a dream," cried Hattie. "My trash *is* on fire."

Cousin Archie fell off the fence in shock! He landed on top of poor Bertie!

"Hurry!" urged Hattie. "We must put the fire out."

All the shouting woke the twins from their dreams.

"Mommy! Mommy!" they meowed, "what's happening?"

Hattie grabbed her kittens and put them on the top of the fence, well away from the dangerous fire.

"You'll be safe here," she told them.

Uncle Bertie knew he had to find some water quickly.

"Over there!" Hattie said, pointing to an old bucket by the fence.

"Hooray!" cried Bertie, finding the bucket half full of water. "It might just be enough to put out the fire."

"Cousin Archie!" he cried. "Come and help me."

The two cats ran down the alley, carrying the bucket between them.

Then, with smoke billowing all around, Archie and Bertie aimed the bucket of water and let go...

111

SPLASH! There was a huge sizzling sound.

"Hooray!" Bertie cried, with a sigh of relief. "We've done it!"

But suddenly, a spark from the fire landed on the trash next to the trash can.

"Oh no, we haven't!" wailed Archie. "Now the trash is on fire!"

"Quick," Hattie said to Archie. "We need more help. Go and wake up the dogs."

At the other end of the alley, the dogs were all fast asleep.

"Help!" shrieked Archie, as he hurtled towards them. "Hattie's trash is on fire. It's spreading down the alley and we can't put it out."

But no one stirred. Archie was always playing tricks on the Alley Dogs and today it was just *too* hot to bother.

Harvey opened one eye lazily.

"That's a good one, Archie," he said. "But you'll have to try harder than that."

"It's true!" Archie shouted, desperately. "Look!"

Harvey sat up slowly.

"This had better not be one of your tricks, Archie," he growled. Then he shaded his eyes from the sun and looked up the alley.

As soon as he saw the billowing smoke, he knew the Alley Cat was telling the truth.

"Archie's right!" barked Harvey. "Quick, everyone to the rescue!"

The dogs raced up the alley towards the fire. Even little Puddles wanted to help. But Harvey scooped her up and placed her on the fence by the kittens.

"You can't do a thing, Puddles!" he said. "Just stay here."

The alley was filled with smelly black smoke. All the cats were coughing and choking. But Harvey knew just what to do.

"Quick!" he said. "Everybody to the water-barrel. Use anything you can to gather the water."

Grabbing old buckets and cans, the cats and dogs formed a long line. Auntie Lucy stood by the barrel to fill up the containers. Then, splishing and splashing, they passed the water along the line to Harvey, who threw it over the fire. Everyone was working really hard.

Suddenly, Lucy gave a cry. "The water's run out!"

"Oh no!" said Archie. "We'll never put the fire out now."

The Alley Cats and Dogs stared in dismay. What could they do? They must have more water.

"Oh, no! We're going to lose our lovely home," wailed Hattie, bursting into tears.

Suddenly, Lenny had an idea.

"I know what to do," he coughed. Grabbing his sister and Puddles, he pulled them over the fence.

"I've just remembered what's in this garden," said Lenny, disappearing into the long grass.

When he came back, he was pulling a hose.

"Mommy!" cried Lenny. "Look what we've got."

Hattie peered through the smoke and gasped. Harvey grabbed the nozzle, as Bertie leapt over the fence and raced to turn the tap on.

With a mighty spurt, the water splashed out, drenching the blazing boxes and soaking the smouldering trash cans. Everyone cheered! Some of the water splashed over the cats and dogs—but they didn't care. The fizzling, sizzling fire was out!

"You little ones deserve a treat for saving our alley!" barked Harvey. "Puppy snacks for you, Puddles, and kitty nibbles for the twins."

"Three cheers for Lenny, Lulu and Puddles!" cried Archie.

"Hip-hip-hooray!"

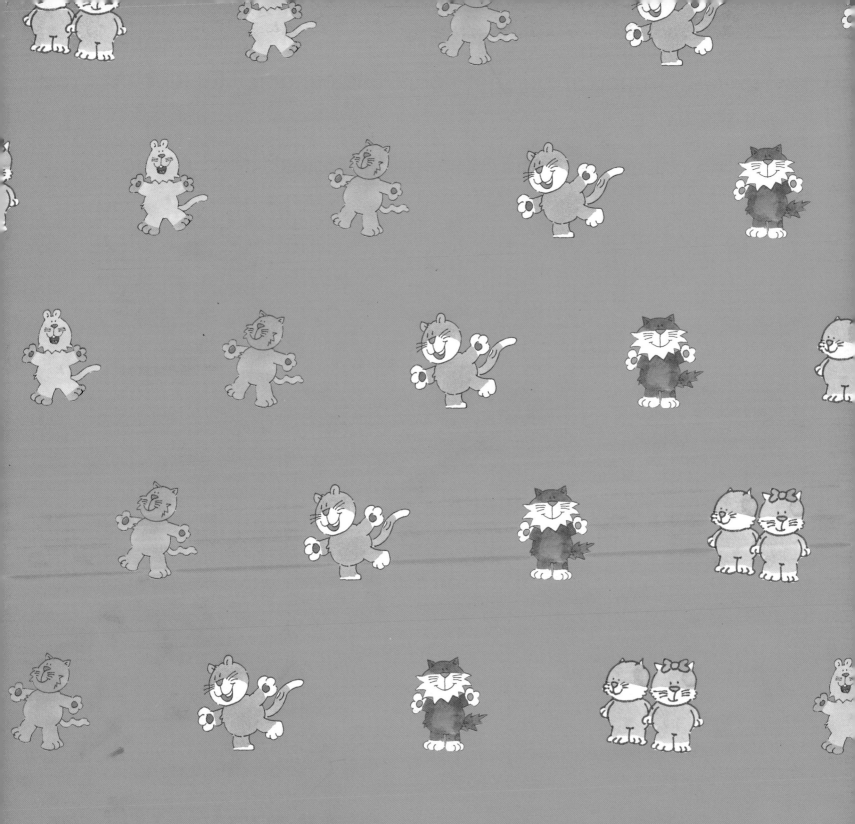